seventeen
trauma-rama

_Life's Most Embarrassing Moments…
and How to Deal_

P9-CAN-895

seventeen
trauma-rama

Life's Most Embarrassing Moments…
and How to Deal

by Megan Stine

A PARACHUTE PRESS BOOK HarperCollins*Publishers*

Created and produced by
PARACHUTE PUBLISHING, L.L.C.
156 Fifth Avenue, Suite 302
New York, New York 10010

Published by
HarperCollins*Publishers*
1350 Avenue of the Americas
New York, New York 10019

Copyright © 2001 PRIMEDIA Magazines Inc., publisher of **seventeen**.
Seventeen is a registered trademark of PRIMEDIA Magazines Finance Inc.

All rights reserved. No part of this book may be used or reproduced in any
manner whatsoever without written permission except in the case of brief
quotations embodied in critical articles or reviews

For information write:
Editorial Manager, **seventeen**
850 Third Avenue
New York, New York 10022

Design by Greg Wozney
Cover illustration by Chuck Gonzales
Printed in Baltimore, Maryland by John D. Lucas Printing

Library of Congress Catalog Card Number: 00-105035

ISBN: 0-06-440873-6

HarperCollins® and ☰® are registered trademarks of HarperCollinsPublishers Inc.

9 8 7 6 5 4 3 2 1

First printing, January 2001

For Pam and Polly—
who have helped me
survive so many traumas

Acknowledgments:

Many thanks to Parachute Publishing, **seventeen** magazine, and HarperCollins Publishers for the opportunity to work on this project; to my editor, Kristen Pettit, for her patience, guidance, enthusiasm, diplomacy, brilliant ideas, and timely solutions; and to Cody Stine for his knowing insights and very generous support. Also, to the many teenagers who shared their most embarrassing moments with me—thank you so much. Your secrets will always be safe.

Table of Contents

HI, AND WELCOME TO TRAUMA-RAMA!

Before you plunge into the world of life's most embarrassing moments, I wanted to give you the scoop on where I got the letters you'll read in this book.

Many of the traumas have come straight from you, the tons of cool **seventeen** readers out there. I also interviewed dozens of teens specifically for this book, and some of these mortifying moments are my own—but please don't ask which ones!

As you read this book, I hope you'll laugh at everyone's mistakes and learn from them, so you won't find yourself in the same position. Or if you do, at least you'll know how to deal.

Keep reading, have fun—and thanks for sending your traumas to **seventeen**. Definitely keep 'em coming!

MEGAN STINE

Life.

Do you ever wonder how you've coped with it so far—and how you'll ever get through the next five minutes, not to mention the next five years?

One thing is for sure, life happens. You wake up in the morning with a new, huge zit…walk into French class totally clueless that your shirt has a huge stain on it…and then bump into the guy you've been crushing on for a month, only to accidentally step on his sprained toe.

In short, you feel like a total loser. You want to scream, "Hey! Who is scripting my life? I demand a rewrite!"

Well, just calm down. We're here for you.

Consider this book your new best friend, your personal trauma-trainer, and your stay-cool coach all rolled into one.

Sure, sometimes life is spelled t-r-a-u-m-a, but you can use several key symbols in this book to help you cope:

TRAUMA
-O-
METER

The trauma-o-meter can help you tell the difference between a brush-it-off blunder, and a change-your-name-and-enter-the-witness-protection-program fiasco. Our rating scale for every trauma in this book goes from 1 (no biggie) to 10 (find a paper bag that will fit nicely over your head). You can use the trauma-o-meter to rate your own traumas, or to flip quickly to the juiciest, most embarrassing moments in this book!

Any section marked with these symbols will show you ways to dodge potential traumas, or deal with them in a way that won't make you look like even more of a loser after they've happened. If you need advice—and fast—be on the lookout for these symbols.

Now that you've got the ground rules down, keep reading. The new smooth and in control you will be happy you did!

Chapter One

Love Bites

Dating Disasters
and How to Avoid Them

As the saying goes, **only fools fall in love**. In other words, once you've fallen in love, you're practically destined to make a complete fool of yourself!

If you aren't dropping French fries all over your date's lap, you're spilling the beans about kissing his best friend last year after the football game.

You're either tripping over your feet—or your tongue. (And we don't even want to *think* about what that means if you're kissing him at the time!)

In short, when it comes to ways to embarrass yourself on dates, the possibilities are endless.

But wouldn't it be fantastic if you could **zap your inner klutz** and figure out how to be your smoothest, coolest self when you're with the guy of your dreams?

It's not that hard. You just have to tap into some basic awareness that **guys aren't the true cause of your Urkel-esque behavior—you are**. That's what this chapter is all about.

Dial-a-Disaster

My dad gave me two tickets to a professional hockey game, and the guy I have a crush on loves sports, so I called him. I said, "I have two free tickets to the hockey game, and I know you love hockey, so I thought you might want to go." He said, "Yeah, great. Just give them to me in bio tomorrow." Then he hung up! I didn't know whether to be embarrassed—or furious. Didn't he know I was asking him for a date?

TRAUMA
-O-
METER

Two words: probably not. And that's gotta hurt, right? It's awful trying to get up the courage to ask out your crush—then striking out big-time.

But fear not! A situation like this doesn't mean the guy you're after doesn't want to hang with you. It just means that guys are slightly less perceptive than girls. (News flash! Like you didn't already know that.)

That's why, when you're asking a guy out, you've got to be totally clear. **You want to hit him over the head with the fact that, yes, you are asking for a date!**

The telephone trauma above could have been easily avoided by the addition of two little words—"with me." As in, "I have hockey tickets and I wondered if you might want to go with me." Now your intentions are totally clear, and your guy can decide if he wants to take you up on your offer or not.

The person who wrote this letter did get one thing absolutely right, however. She started off on the right foot by choosing to use the telephone. Of course, it's fine to ask for a date in person, but let's face it: If you're *rejected* in person, the trauma factor increases mathematically by a thousand.

Check out the beauty of asking someone out over the phone on our list on the next page.

THREE
Crucial Reasons to Use
THE PHONE

❶ Privacy. You—and he—won't have anyone else hanging around, intruding on the big moment. You *could* go up to him in the hall or during lunch at school, but you're going to have an audience for that. Half the school will be watching, waiting to see whether he says yes or no. And if there's one thing most guys don't like, it's playing out their private lives in public. Stick to the phone. He's more likely to say yes if his friends aren't breathing down his neck at the time.

❷ The Hot Seat. Your crush can't get distracted or walk away in the middle of your question, the way he can in a face-to-face encounter, if you call him on the phone. And he can't fake a sudden computer failure the way he can if you e-mail him. On the phone, he's a captive audience—bound to give you some kind of answer before he hangs up.

❸ The Cheat Sheet. It's easier to remember all the things you want to say to your crush if you write them down. Time, date, place, transportation, names of other friends who might be joining you—all the key date info could go onto your cheat sheet. Then, if your crush says, "A movie on Saturday? Cool. What time?" you'll be right there with the answer because you planned it out and wrote it down in advance.

Smash Potatoes

At camp last summer, I met the guy of my dreams. One day, to get him to notice me, I just happened to walk by his table during dinner. As I went by carrying my plate of food, I casually looked over my shoulder to grin at him. He smiled back at me and then—whack! I walked into a pole and spilled the entire plate of mashed potatoes on my brand-new black shirt. When I looked around, the entire mess hall was laughing—including my crush. I ran out, totally humiliated.

TRAUMA -O- METER

We can just imagine the look on his face—and the sinking feeling in your chest.

Here's a statistic that's just *has* to be true, even if there isn't a load of scientific research to back it up: **ninety percent of all klutzy behavior in front of guys is due to nerves**.

Just think back. You tripped and fell in front of your dream machine...or felt so tongue-tied that you couldn't spell your own name if your life depended on it...or dropped your books so they went flying at his kneecaps...or dribbled salsa down the front of your new white silk shirt.

And why? No other reason except that *he* was there. The guy with the unbelievably cute spiky hair and smile that could melt M&Ms in your hand. Yup—he was there, and suddenly you turned into a world-class klutz.

There isn't much you can do if your nervous system goes into spasm mode whenever your favorite hottie is within fifty feet. **But you can do a few things to minimize the damage**.

COOL RULES

How to Avoid Acting Klutzy in Front of Guys

1. Don't eat or drink anything around him until you've gotten past that so-nervous-you-want-to-jump-out-of-your-skin phase. The fewer liquids in your hands, the better the chances that you'll survive your encounter without an embarrassing boost to your dry-cleaning bill.

2. Try to hold still. Seriously, we know you're excited to be around him, but try not to twirl your hair, swing your foot, break into a tap routine, or twitch in any way. For one thing, guys aren't generally as wired as we are, so they're more comfortable around girls who aren't bouncing off the walls. And if you are able to stay still, you're less likely to trip, fall, or do an unintentional somersault, making a complete spectacle of yourself.

3. Take a deep breath and slow down. Think meditation. Think Zen. Try to project an inner calm—even if you don't feel it. If you keep reminding yourself that there's no rush, you're less likely to stumble through those precious moments with your main crush.

For two months I'd been trying to get this guy's attention. I kept saying things like "We should go to the movies sometime," and I'd name movies I hadn't seen yet. Finally he called me up and said, "I'm taking you up on your offer. You want to go see the new basketball flick?" I was thrilled—until we got to the box office. He didn't have any money and thought I was going to treat. But I thought we were paying for ourselves. I had only enough money for me! We were both so embarrassed, we haven't spoken since.

Whoops. **Don't pass go, don't collect $200** (although you could have used it at the box office!), and *do* pay *close* attention to Chapter Two, "Message Madness."

The main deal here is that **both people had a form of DD—dating dyslexia.** Everyone read all the signals backward. She invited him to the movies but didn't make it clear that it wasn't her treat. His question—"You want to go see the new basketball flick?"—sure *sounded* like he was asking her out. But the part about taking her up on her offer definitely confused the issue.

So what now? If you don't know an usher who can let you sneak into the movies for free, you're going to have to be creative. First, fess up to your total mortification. That usually works to put your date at ease. Say something like **"I'm so embarrassed!** I thought we'd each pay for ourselves, but I guess we should have talked about it earlier."

Then move quickly on to step two: Suggest something fun that you can do together *without* spending big bucks. Don't let the date fall flat over something as trivial as money.

Offer to rent an *old* basketball film and watch it at your house—and of course the microwave popcorn is on you! Or hang out in the parking lot and quiz people about the movie as they come out, just for kicks.

In other words, come up with something fun to save the situation, and he'll soon forget that he wanted to melt into the pavement.

The guy I'd been going with for a year left town with his family for Christmas vacation. I was really lonely and didn't want to spend the holidays by myself, so when another guy asked me out, I accepted. When my main man called, my little sister told him I was out on a date. Busted!

TRAUMA -O- METER

Naturally, **you don't want to spend New Year's Eve ice fishing with your dad**, or playing Frisbee in the snow with your dog. But is that any reason to betray the sweetie who bought you those adorable fuzzy mittens and matching hat, made a CD with all your favorite Christmas carols on it, and nicknamed you his "snow angel"?

Or, to put it another way, **how would you feel if he cheated on you that way**?

If you think all's fair in love and war, check out the Cool Rules on the following page.

It's more than just embarrassing to be caught two-timing your honey. It's downright **WRONG**.

All's Fair in Love and War? Not Quite.

SITUATION	FAIR	UNFAIR
Your best friend has it bad for the new guy in school. She's been drooling over him for two weeks, but he hasn't noticed her yet.	Go out with him if he asks you—but clear it with your BF first.	Turn on the turbojets and chase after him like there's no tomorrow.
Your main man leaves town for the summer.	Tell him in advance that you think you both ought to be free to date other people while he's gone.	Figure what he doesn't know won't hurt him, and spend two weeks kissing his best friend at the beach.
You've been seeing two different guys at the same time.	Tell them both that you're not ready to be committed.	Let each of them think he's the one whose name you're scribbling in your spiral notebook.
One of your close friends breaks it off with her guy. You've always thought he was a hottie.	Talk to her about how she'd feel if the two of you dated. Then before you go after him, let a few weeks go by to make sure she doesn't change her mind.	Without talking to your friend, go after her ex full-speed-ahead before the two of them have a chance to patch it up and get back together.

Does He Really Like You?

He's giving you signals...but what do they mean? Find out *before* you make a fool of yourself!

1. The cutie in your bio class hasn't actually talked to you much. But each day when class is over, he usually:

  a) leaves as quickly as possible since his next class is way on the other side of school.

  b) strolls to the door, leaving lots of bump-into-each-other opportunities.

  c) flirts with the new French exchange student.

2. You and your latest crush are paired for a civics project, and you're supposed to get together outside of class to make plans. He suggests:

  a) that you call him sometime so you can talk about it over the phone.

  b) that you can probably figure it out fast in the hallway between classes.

  c) that the two of you should go to the library tonight and, come to think of it, he'll give you a ride if you need one.

3. You're standing behind the guy you're crushing on in the cafeteria line, waiting to get your lunch trays. His body language is:

  a) closed—he keeps his back to you the whole time, never turning around once.

b) uncertain—he stands sideways so you can see his big baby blues while he clowns around with his friends.

c) open—he's practically facing you the whole time, teasing you about how nasty the food is going to be since it's Sloppy Joe Day.

4. His locker is near yours in the hall, which means you're always around while he's:

a) flirting with the redhead whose homeroom is across the hall.

b) teasing you about how messy your locker is—stuffed with empty soda cans and homework papers.

c) bragging to his friends about how many points he scored last night in his favorite video game.

5. When you run into him at the movies, he and his buds sit:

a) behind you.

b) beside you.

c) in front of you.

6. You invent an excuse to call him about a math homework assignment, pretending you've forgotten which problems to do. He:

a) tells you the assignment matter-of-factly and then hangs up.

b) launches into a discussion about how ugly your math teacher's ties are.

c) gives you the assignment and then can't think of anything else to say.

7. You casually mention to your main crush that you and your best bud, Carly, are going to the varsity basketball game tomorrow night. When you get there, you notice that:

a) your crush came with just one friend, too—his sidekick, Ben.

b) he showed up with a gang of guys.

c) he's a no-show.

8. On Valentine's Day, you hurry to American history class so you can leave a "secret admirer" card on his desk. When he finds it, he:

a) stuffs it in his backpack with an embarrassed look on his face.

b) immediately glances over at you with a question in his eyes.

c) crumples it up and throws it away.

Add up your answers and then check out your score on the following pages.

1.	(a)2	(b)3	(c)1
2.	(a)2	(b)1	(c)3
3.	(a)1	(b)2	(c)3
4.	(a)1	(b)3	(c)2
5.	(a)2	(b)3	(c)1
6.	(a)1	(b)3	(c)2
7.	(a)3	(b)2	(c)1
8.	(a)2	(b)3	(c)1

Signs Point to Yes (20–24 points)

No doubt about it—your guy is interested. He hangs around after class, clowns around near your locker, and teases you in the lunch line for a reason. You're the audience he most wants to impress. (Really, we can't figure out what's taking him so long to ask you out!) So go ahead and make the first move yourself. Try something supersafe—like asking him for a study date, or offering to share your dessert at lunch. With signals like these, he won't need an antenna to read your message loud and clear.

Ask Again Later (14–19 points)

Your secret crush has a few secrets of his own—and they're hard to figure out. Does he go suddenly silent on the phone because he's shy? Intimidated? Or just bored? Is he hoping you'll make the first move—or are you not even on his radar screen? It's hard to tell with guys who send mixed messages. Try to find out if he's interested by being a little more direct. Mention that you and some friends are taking in the midnight horror flicks at the Cineplex, and suggest, "Maybe you should come along." If he's been hoping for a chance like this, he'll leap at it. Otherwise, you may have to admit that he's a cute package—but not crush-able.

My Sources Say No (8–13 points)

Chances are this guy's head and heart are elsewhere. If he's making time for everyone but you, it's probably not some kind of complicated Cruel Intentions ploy to make you jealous and turn your head. He's just not interested—not now anyway. But who knows? Maybe someday he'll come to his senses and realize what an amazing person you are—or at least wake up to the fact that you've got some killer ideas for that civics project! In the meantime, you're better off finding another cutie to focus your energy on.

Chapter Two

Message Madness

How to Avoid Making a Complete Fool of Yourself in Phone Calls, Letters, Notes, E-mail, and Especially Face-to-Face

You're standing in line with your new boyfriend at a school potluck dinner, trying to fill your plate from the buffet table. **"Ewww,"** you mutter, wrinkling up your nose at a particular dish on the table. **"What's that? It looks nasty!"**

"It's tabouli Mexicana," your new guy snaps. "And my mom made it."

Whoops!

Let's face it. There is a whole slew of potentially embarrassing moments lurking out there in the world, but the worst embarrassment of all can come from your very own lips. It's the things you say—or don't know how to say—that often leave you feeling like you've just shoved a Chicago Bulls–sized shoe into your mouth. (Not too tasty!)

When you're nervous, you're more likely to either blurt out the wrong thing—or, worse, be unable to think of anything to say.

But don't panic. You *can* **vaccinate yourself against foot-in-mouth disease**. Just check out the guidelines in this chapter, and you'll soon be more talkative than a first-grader on a sugar high.

While keeping an eye on my younger sis at the community pool, I happened to notice a sexy swimmer doing flips off the diving platform. I almost passed out when he actually came over to talk to me. But even more surprising was that he spoke to me in Polish, which I coincidentally know. He was wondering if the girl I was watching was my sister, but I was so flustered that I responded, "Yes, my daughter." One look at his terrified expression and my major mistake dawned on me. Needless to say, he didn't hang around.

TRAUMA
-O-
METER

Mistakenly identifying yourself as a teenage mom can be pretty embarrassing, but we gave this one a low trauma rating because of the foreign language factor. It's hard enough talking to guys—but in a second language? *¡Ay caramba!*

But no matter what language she's speaking, every girl has been there—**you open your mouth and nothing comes out**. Or, worse, you stumble around, trying to find the right thing to say—and hear yourself babbling an unending string of vowels. (For example: **"I-uuuuuuuuhh-uuuummmmmm."**)

Listen, learning to talk to people in general, and guys in particular, isn't rocket science. It's all a matter of getting your mind-set right—and following these four COOL RULES for talking to guys.

How to Talk to Guys in Four Easy Steps

1. Pick a topic ahead of time. Planning ahead is key when you know you're going to be nervous. If you're going to be in the company of the guy of your dreams and you know he's into sports, plan to ask him if he'd rather play or watch the pros—and then ask him why. (Don't forget to ask why—you'll see why in Rule #3 below.) If sports aren't his thing, choose another topic that he'll be into: music, movies, school, college choices, summer jobs, vacations, whatever—and have a question ready in advance. Asking if he's seen the latest blockbuster movie is a great default question—and always good for starters. And don't forget to have a back-up topic handy to fill in the gaps if the first topic falls flat.

2. Focus on the other person, not on yourself. Try to remember that the guy you're with is probably just as nervous as you are— then strive to put him at ease. Be friendly, relaxed, and open. If he likes that big blockbuster movie you mentioned, ask him what his favorite scene was. Which leads to our next very important point...

3. Ask questions that require more than a one-word answer. Hey, your main crush might feel just as tongue-tied as you do. So if you ask him a question that can be answered with just one word, that's exactly what you're likely to get. Instead, keep him talking. Try to come up with a subject that requires some explanation. For example, "My friends and I were joking around yesterday, talking about the three things we'd take with us if we ended up stranded on a desert island. So what would you take?" It's a gimmicky conversation-starter—but it works.

4. **When in doubt, ask more questions.** Admit it—you want to know everything about this guy—especially if you've been ogling him for months. So ask! Where did he go to kindergarten? Are his parents together? Does he have a little brother? Is he a morning person or a night owl? Vegetarian or junk food fanatic? Does he hate the Backstreet Boys—or wish he could be one of them? Just keep firing questions at him. It will keep the conversation going. And, as a bonus, once you've heard all the answers, you'll have an idea about whether or not you two really click.

A group of us were at a party where we met some guys from a different school. They introduced themselves, but I didn't catch all their names. Later that night, my best friend arrived. One of the guys came over to flirt. My friend obviously wanted me to introduce him to her, but I couldn't remember his name. I didn't know what to say, so I just stood there saying, "This is...uhhh...uhhhh..." He wouldn't help me out, so finally I just turned around and walked away. I felt so dumb.

TRAUMA -o- METER

Introduction Amnesia. It's the most common mistake people make, especially when they're meeting and greeting for the first time. You're so eager for the other person to meet you—to hear your name, check out your smile—you totally forget to listen to *his* name and hopefully connect it with *his* smile the next time you see him. It can really get embarrassing, too, if the next time you need to remember his name is only five minutes later!

Here's our hint for remembering the name of someone you just met—look the person straight in the eye, and address him or her *using his or her name*. (Example: "Hi, *Tim*. Nice to meet you.") Using someone's name right away will help you to remember it later.

Even with that helpful hint, let's face it, meeting someone for the first time is stressful and intimidating. But you can check out the LIFE SAVERS chart for coping with introductions. These rules will help you cover all the meet-and-greet bases.

LIFE SAVERS for Introductions

Situation	What to say
You forget someone's name even after you've been introduced.	Be honest here. Say something like "Oh, my gosh! Sorry, I'm so terrible with names. Could you tell me yours again?"
You want to talk to someone you don't know.	Introduce yourself by saying, "Hi, I'm (your name here)." Then pause long enough for the other person to give you his name. Even if he doesn't, ask the person something that will tell you more about him like, "Are you friends with Mark?" or "Are you new at this school?" Or you can practically force him to give you his name by saying, "You're Jeremy, right?"
You need to introduce a new acquaintance to your friend, but you can't remember your acquaintance's name.	There are two ways to tackle this one. *The honest approach:* Turn to her and say, "Come meet Jason—I think you two will like each other. Oh, and tell me your name again?" *The hedge-your-bets approach:* Say, "Oh, I'd like you to meet someone. This is my friend Jason." Then cross your fingers and hope your acquaintance picks up the ball and introduces herself to your friend.
You're introducing a friend to your parents or another adult.	Always introduce the younger person to the older one, to show respect. For instance, say, "Mom, I'd like you to meet Kevin. He's a model and MTV veejay I just met." (You wish!)

I went out with a new guy while I was still sort of seeing my old boyfriend. Neither of them knew about the other. Then, one night, my beeper went off with a message from my best girlfriend. The new guy saw the message, which read: "Which guy are you with now???" I know she meant it as a joke—for my eyes only—but it was pretty embarrassing.

TRAUMA
-O-
METER

Sure, technology rocks. **Who doesn't love cell phones**, answering machines, and pagers? They're great ninety-eight percent of the time, but they're also the source of uber-embarrass-ment when they leak information at the wrong time. Or when they butt in on a private moment that should have been between you and that gorgeous guy who finally asked you out after you flirted with him for three months.

That's why you've got to **be careful of who's around** when you check your messages, read your beeper, or even answer your cell phone. If Guy 1 calls while you're getting a mocha with Guy 2, someone's going to figure out what's going on and get his feelings hurt. Better to leave your techno-toys turned off while you're on a date. After all, you wouldn't bring another guy along and make it a threesome, would you?

And while we're at it, here are a few more **TIPS** for the world of cyber-speak

COOL RULES

Telephone Techno-Talk Tips: Dos and Don'ts

▼ **DON'T** put private phone calls on a speakerphone so your friends can listen in. For that matter, don't let them eavesdrop on your phone calls at all without letting all parties know about it.

▼ **DON'T** check your answering machine or voice mail with casual friends in the room. What if you get a message inviting you to a party and they're not included? They'll be hurt and embarrassed. On the other hand, if you get a call from your soccer coach, chewing you out about missing four practices, you'll be the one with the red face. So keep personal messages personal.

▼ **DO** turn off your cell phone on dates and whenever the ringing could annoy people. (Do you really want the entire audience glaring at you when your phone rings during the final, scariest moments of *Scream 5*?)

There's this guy I talk to on-line and everything between us has been great, so I decided to tell my best friend about it. I wrote how much I liked him, then copied and pasted me and my "pal's" conversation into an e-mail and sent it to my girlfriend. Well, silly me, I accidentally sent it to the guy's e-mail address instead! I never felt so humiliated in all my life!

Yikes. We feel your pain.

If there's one thing that guys hate, it's girls who get ahead of them in the commitment department. Telling a guy you really like him before he's ready to hear it is a surefire relationship killer. But guess what will douse the flames of passion even faster? Putting those feelings out there for all the world to scope out.

Face it, if you're carrying a flame for someone in your heart, no one has to know about it but you. But when you put it in writing, others can see it—and hold you to it.

When it comes to love letters, there's only one COOL RULE that counts: *Don't send one until you're extra extra sure of your guy's feelings for you.* And that goes for notes to friends in which you declare your everlasting adoration for your main crush, too. Because **what you put in writing could get into the wrong hands.** You may have to live with your words— or live them down!—for the rest of your life.

What else should never be put in writing? (Except in your journal, of course.) Plenty!

▼ Plans to break up with your guy

▼ Details of your latest make-out session

▼ Someone else's secrets

▼ Gossip and rumors

▼ Anger or other strong emotions that you may mellow about in a day or two

▼ Anything that would seriously change your life if your parents read it

Chapter Three

Fear of Food!

How to Get Through Any Meal Gracefully—and That's the Best Dessert of All

Do you dread an encounter with a plate of spaghetti? Break into a cold sweat at the thought of the lineup of forks at your best friend's brother's wedding? Wonder what's the right way to act in a fancy restaurant?

Well, you're not alone. Nobody wants to sit down to a nice meal and have someone shoot them a look that says, **"Who raised you—wolves?"**

Relax. Food can be challenging...but all you need to do is show it who's boss. Read on. You're guaranteed to breeze through this crash course in eating etiquette!

Last summer I was invited to go with a friend and her family to a resort they visit every year. We ate dinner each night in the formal, fancy dining room. It was hard enough trying to figure out which fork to use for the salad, which for the dessert, etc. But the worst moment came when the waiter brought little bowls of clear liquid with lemon slices floating in them. I thought it was some kind of cold, lemony soup, so I picked up my spoon and started to eat it. That's when my friend's mother explained that it was a finger bowl—something you use to clean your greasy fingers! I wanted to die of embarrassment.

TRAUMA -o- METER

Okay—that's ugly. Drinking something that you were supposed to dip your dirty fingers in is pretty embarrassing. But the good news is that once you've been-there-done-that, you're not likely to make the same mistake again— not with the finger bowl anyway. More likely, you'll find yourself dangling your fingers in the next bowl of clear whatever that a waiter puts in front of you—only to find out it's chicken broth!

So what's a girl to do?

Luckily, there's a very simple, very elegant COOL RULE that can get you through any fancy dinner party and avoid those oh-my-God-I-want-to-die moments. And here it is:

When in doubt, watch the hostess (in the case above, your friend's mom), **then do whatever she does**.

Easy, right? Let's say you're facing an array of forks large enough to supply a small village. Which one do you use? Check out the one your hostess picks up *before* choosing your weapon.

Don't know whether or not to pick up that rack of lamb by the bone and nibble away? See what plan of attack your hostess chooses. Even if she's not correct according to Miss Manners, you'll be in the clear. See, it's the hostess's party—and she can double-dip if she wants to.

As for some basic rules around the table—here's the short list.

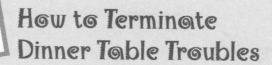

How to Terminate Dinner Table Troubles

1. At a small dinner, never begin eating until everyone is served and the hostess begins.

2. At a large party (like a wedding, bar mitzvah, or gigantic family reunion), go ahead and start when the two or three people seated nearest you have their food as well. Don't wait for everyone, or your veggie lasagna will turn into a gross, gelatinous lump.

3. Use the silverware in order, from the outside in. (This really works—unless the table hasn't been properly set. In which case, you're not to blame!) So if you follow this rule and still find you're stuck eating the main course with a teeny-tiny shrimp fork, just quietly ask a waiter or the hostess for a fork and go on as if nothing has happened.

4. Put your napkin in your lap as soon as you sit down. Place it on your chair if you leave the table—to go to the rest room, for instance. (Don't put a dirty napkin on a table where people are still eating. Yuck!) Leave your napkin on the table when dinner is over.

I went out with my crush and his parents to an Italian restaurant, and everyone was ordering spaghetti, so I did too. I thought that the waiter would bring big spoons to help us twirl the spaghetti, but he didn't. I ended up slurping long, dangling pieces of spaghetti and getting sauce all over my blouse, while his parents stared at me like I was a barbarian.

TRAUMA
-0-
METER

That's rough. Especially because you didn't mean to be messy! Unfortunately, some foods are just loaded with embarrassment potential. For instance, spaghetti—did you know they never serve it at White House state dinners?

Like most dangerous foods, spaghetti looks so innocent—until you dig in. Then, before you know it, you're slinging Alfredo sauce in every direction, or struggling to capture those longer-than-you-thought-and-rapidly-unwinding strands. Not a pretty sight.

So what are you supposed to do when you're faced with a plate full of stringy pasta? The truth is, if you're going with the straight etiquette deal, you twirl it onto your fork while it's still on your plate. But different families and different parts of the country follow different customs. For instance, many Italian people use the spoon-aid method. So go with the flow. If the family you're dining with happens to favor wrapping it around their fingers and then biting it off—well, go for it. You can stand it for one night, and you'll be out of there soon enough!

But, if you have a choice, the smartest route is to try to avoid the down-and-dirty, messy foods that are likely to leave you wearing half your dinner on your shirt. Translation: *Don't order the spaghetti!* Order the penne, ziti, or ravioli, which can be handled in individual bites instead.

If there's no way out, then follow these LIFE SAVERS that will get you through even the most perilous picnic or dangerous dining experience.

 # Life Savers for Eating Difficult Foods

MESSY FOOD	THE PROBLEM	LIFE-SAVER SOLUTION
Spaghetti	Dangling and escaping strands, with flying bits of sauce that end up on your clothes—or someone else's!	Twirl very small amounts on your fork. Make sure you've got it under control before lifting to your mouth.
Ice Cream Cone	Melts faster than you can eat it. Then it drips all over you. Or drips through the tiny hole in the bottom of the cone.	Order ice cream in a cup on scorcher days. If the hole's the problem, ask the counter person to drop a mini marshmallow in the bottom of the cone. Voila! Instant drip protector!
Fried Chicken	The big question: to use your fingers, or not to use your fingers?	Pick it up and eat it with your fingers at a picnic. Use the very tip of your knife to pierce the crusty batter when at a dinner table. Then use your fork to enjoy the meal.

MESSY FOOD	THE PROBLEM	LIFE-SAVER SOLUTION
Corn on the cob	Greasy, slippery, and you get kernels stuck in your teeth.	If everyone else is eating it, why shouldn't you? Just remember to remove stray corn that's stuck in your teeth in private. (That's not a sight you want your friends to see!)
Sub sandwich, grinder, or hero	Ingredients become more slippery as you eat, the tomato starts sliding out, and pretty soon you've got mayo all over your hands and face.	Cut the offending sandwich into smaller, more manageable pieces and eat them one at a time—or leave the paper wrapper partly wrapped around the sandwich to hold it all together
Pizza	Large slices tend to droop, and the stringy cheese won't let go.	Eat it with a knife and fork until it's half gone. Then go ahead and pick it up. Order the crust extra-crispy to reduce floppage.
Lobster	The undisputed heavyweight champion in the messy foods department. The liquid drips all over, bits of juice fly around the room, and you've got to use your hands to excavate all the yummy meat.	Why do you think they usually give out bibs in lobster restaurants? Wear it—and everyone else will too. (If you're the only one who ordered lobster, face it—you're going to be the entertainment for the evening.)

MESSY FOOD	THE PROBLEM	LIFE-SAVER SOLUTION
Nachos	Lots of opportunities to drip salsa, sour cream, or bits of ground beef all over the table before the bite ever reaches your mouth.	Ask the waiter or hostess for small plates for each person, and serve individual portions. That way the food has less distance to travel. Translation: less chance to make a mess.
Fresh peaches or plums	One bite and—if they're ripe—you've got juice dripping down your chin.	Hold a paper napkin in your hand, under the fruit, when you bite into it.
BBQ ribs	Just a lot of stickiness and finger licking. And your face is in your food—literally—through the whole meal. Better hope there are no photographers handy.	Most restaurants will bring bibs and/or wet wipes to help you cope with the mess. But eating ribs is an exhibition sport—so don't order this unless other people do. Then dig in and enjoy!

Cash Crunch

My date and I went to a really nice (and expensive!) restaurant for dinner before the prom. He said I should order anything I wanted, so I did. I ordered the lobster tails, plus an appetizer and dessert—even though he ordered only a main course. When the check came, he was really embarrassed because he was two dollars short. I lent him the money, but I felt like a fool—especially when he said, "Sorry, I just didn't think you'd eat so much!"

Sounds like a dinner disaster—with no one going home happy. But maybe you're thinking: Wasn't this the guy's fault? He *told* her to order whatever she wanted, right?

True. But it's best to listen to everything else your date has to say—to the subtle clues guys give out. Sure, he said, **"Order anything you want."** That was guy-speak for "I'm trying to show you a great time, and I want you to think I've got this all under control."

Also, he might have spoken before he'd checked out the prices on the menu. Or maybe he didn't think he'd be taken so literally.

Whatever the case, it's always a good idea to let your date in on what you're planning to order. Say something like "When you said order whatever I want, did you mean it? Because I'm thinking of having the shrimp cocktail and the prime rib." Then watch his reaction carefully and try to follow his lead.

What else do you need to know about sailing through a hot dinner-date without winding up in the soup?

Cool Rules for Restaurant Rendezvous

1. **Who orders?** In the Dark Ages, the guy did the ordering for both people on a date. But, really, in the post-Jurassic age, you're allowed to use your own mouth. Tell the waiter what you want, and feel free to ask questions. If you hate scallions, it's much better to find out that the salad is loaded with them before it arrives.

2. **What if the waiter is snooty?** There's not much you can do about waiters who give you decent service but lace it with a heavy dose of attitude—although you can choose another restaurant next time. But if the waiter treats you like a second-class customer—ignoring you for long periods, for instance (maybe because you're younger than the rest of the crowd)—you don't have to stand for it. Get up and tell the host, the maitre d', or manager about the problem. If the waiter doesn't shape up, you can also give him some serious feedback when it's time to leave a tip.

3. **What if it's an unfamiliar cuisine?** Don't know how to use chopsticks? Can't translate the French menu? Don't panic—just tell your date the truth. Fess up that you're new to the experience, and let someone with practice be your guide.

   Chopsticks aren't hard to use, but you probably don't want to learn on a date, or your maki could end up in your date's lap. So ask for a fork. If you and your date/friends find yourselves staring blankly at a menu written in Slovakian, ask the waiter for help. Otherwise, you may wind up eating a plateful of brains—which won't make you feel very smart.

4. **What if you hate your food?** Send it back. Let's say you've ordered fettuccine Alfredo and the noodles arrive swimming in a deep pool of cheesy grease. You take one look and think, No way. Simply catch the waiter's eye, and when he comes over say, "Excuse me, but this has more oil than I expected. May I order something else?" Most restaurants are quite willing to let you send back food you're not happy with. If the waiter gives you undue hassle, see Rule 2.

5. **Who pays?** On a date, you pay if you asked him out. He pays if he did the inviting. Whoever isn't shelling out for dinner ought to cough up some cash for the tip, or buy gelatos on the way home.

If you've been seeing the same guy for a while, the two of you should take turns financing the fun. But when you're out on the town with three of your buds, it's easiest if you just split the check four ways. Don't get into adding up who had the chicken and who had the fish unless it's really uneven—say, if someone ordered steak and someone else had only a salad.

Don't forget to add at least 15 percent for the tip, 20 percent for better service, or when there's a large staff of people serving you.

Someone dropped a greasy piece of pepperoni on a chair in the caf, but I didn't notice, so I sat down there. When I got up, I had this huge bull's-eye right in the middle of my back-side! Everyone was laughing so hard. Even after I brushed it off, I was still left with a hideous, round grease stain.

TRAUMA
-O-
METER

Like we said before, life happens. You can't fall apart every time you spill cola on your jeans or drip nacho cheese on your favorite top. But having a great big stain right in the middle of one breast, or smack on your backside, can be pretty embarrassing. At times like that, you've got two choices: Clean up the stain, or live with it till you get home.

If you can't remove the stain, **try to forget it**. If someone points it out to you, don't act embarrassed. Just say, "Oh, that. Yeah. **I sat on a piece of pepperoni**." The less you make of any spots, the less people will put you on the spot for it.

If you can't ignore the stain, try to joke about it. Tell your friends, "I'm marking the spots where I need to lose weight." Or "I don't know how that got there—**some guy must have been drooling!**" The more embarrassing the blob, the more outrageous your comeback line should be.

Are You Dinner-Date Material?

Some people are just too embarrassing to eat dinner with in public. Are you one of them?

1. You and your latest crush decide to get a pizza and study together. You're most likely to order:

a) whatever he wants.

b) veggie pizza with broccoli, red onions, and roasted red peppers on one half, mushrooms and extra cheese on the other half—but only if the mushrooms are fresh, not canned; and light on the tomato sauce, please!

c) you're easy—you like mushrooms and pepperoni, but you're fine with plain cheese too.

2. At dinner before the prom, you drop your fork a few minutes into the meal. You:

a) ask the waiter for another one.

b) eat your fried shrimp with your fingers, holding them by the tails, and just skip the baked potato.

c) ask your date to give you his fork so you can keep eating, and make him get a clean one from the staff.

3. The guy who sits behind you in English asks if you want to go out for burgers after the basketball game. You're a vegetarian, so you:

a) quiz the waitress about every item on the menu, then complain that they ought to serve tofu burgers, and finally settle for a glass of water, which disappoints you because it has too much ice.

b) order French fries and tell him you're not very hungry, worrying that he won't like you if he finds out you're a selective eater.

c) bring your own munchies—carrot sticks and sliced jicama—in case they don't serve anything you can eat, and order honey-mustard sauce to dip them in.

4. You and your main guy are celebrating your six-month anniversary by having dinner out. He's picked a fun-casual restaurant with a huge menu and a gazillion choices. You:

a) glance at the entrees and appetizers until you spot two of your faves—fried mozzarella sticks and teriyaki chicken—then order those.

b) debate out loud for ten minutes about whether to have soup or salad, wonder if the stir-fry is any good, and change your mind twice after you've already given your order.

c) can't make up your mind what to order until you know what he's ordering.

5. You invite the cute new guy at school to go out for a latté. When it's time to pay, you:

a) hang back, expecting him to offer to pay.

b) pull out your money cheerfully and ask the clerk how much you owe.

c) pay for him, but feel weird about it, wondering if he shouldn't have paid for himself.

6. The guy of your dreams asks you to eat lunch with him in the caf. Once the two of you are up-close-and-personal, you realize he could use a few tips about table manners. For one thing, he holds his spoon like a shovel. You:

a) let it slide—you're not trying to be his mother.
b) feel relieved and identify, because you hold your spoon strangely too.
c) point out his mistakes seriously—but jokingly—and hope he changes.

7. You've been seeing the same guy for four months and his parents want to meet you. They invite you to a family dinner on Sunday night. Your biggest fear is:

a) you could be late, since you'll be coming straight from a basketball game.
b) dinner will run too long—and you and he will miss watching the MTV movie awards.
c) they'll serve something with tomatoes, which always make you break out in hives.

8. You're on a diet, but the senior guy you've been crushing on finally asks you out for a late-night snack at an all-night waffle house. You:

a) order a glass of OJ and a piece of dry toast, casually explaining that you're not very hungry.
b) order the most expensive thing on the menu since he's paying.
c) turn down the offer because you're afraid if you go, you'll be tempted to binge.

1.	(a)1	(b)3	(c)2
2.	(a)2	(b)1	(c)3
3.	(a)3	(b)1	(c)2
4.	(a)2	(b)1	(c)3
5.	(a)3	(b)2	(c)1
6.	(a)1	(b)1	(c)3
7.	(a)2	(b)3	(c)1
8.	(a)2	(b)3	(c)1

2222211 2

14

2212211 2

Add up your answers and read your scores below.

Over Easy (8–11 points)

You might gag at the sight of green peppers, but no one will ever know it because you're determined to be a low-maintenance date. It's fine to be easygoing, but you just might be overdoing it in the "whatever you want" department. Remember that no guy wants to date himself. He asked you to dinner to find out who you are, so give him a chance. Go out on a limb and order your own pizza toppings for a change. You'll be happy to find out that he can probably handle it even if you're a roasted garlic and onions girl all the way.

Table for Two (12–19 points)

No guy should have reservations about taking you to dinner. Whether it's a five-course meal at the Ritz or burgers and fries at the corner café, you're perfectly at ease. You've put food in its place and figured out that it's not so much about what you eat— it's about spending some quality face time with friends and getting to know the people you're with. You've also got enough poise to handle it if your chicken arrives burned, or they're out of your favorite dessert. So what are you doing Friday at eight?

Food Critic—No Stars (20–24 points)

If the waiter forgets that you asked for the salad dressing on the side, watch out. You're not only sure of what you want, you'll throw a small fit if you don't get it. Knowing your own mind is great, but how about taking some time to chill and enjoying yourself a little? If you're fussing over what to order and complaining when they don't bring enough dinner rolls, it doesn't leave much room for a good time. Try to let go of the reins once in a while. You might even find you like the honey-mustard vinaigrette that was brought to you by mistake better than what you ordered!

Chapter Four

Clothes Call!

Not Even the Fashion Police Can Arrest These Disasters

You've spent three hours getting ready. Bought the perfect white jeans and blue top. Worked on your hair until it's just the way you like it.

You're totally psyched for your big date—miniature golfing with the guy of your dreams. And you've put in so much mirror time, you wonder **what could possibly go wrong?**

The sad truth is—plenty!

Suddenly, when you least expect it, you've got a soft drink spilled all over you, a sleeve ripped off, or, worse—something showing that was never meant to be seen in public.

At that moment, your face is so red, you could **camouflage yourself with a stop sign!**

But, hey, fashion disasters occur. The trick is in knowing how to **prevent some of them**—and **cope with the rest**.

I decided to wear a skirt to school one day—instead of my usual jeans. After the fourth-period bell rang, I picked up my heavy backpack, hauled the strap over my shoulder, and headed to the chorus room. On my way, I saw this really hot senior I'd been eyeing since forever. I walked a little faster, hoping to catch up to him so I could pass by and say hi. But as I did, I heard him and his friends snickering. I wondered why, until I got to the chorus room and my best friend said, "Your skirt is caught in your book bag and your underwear is showing." Oh, no!

TRAUMA
-0-
METER

It's happened to all of us. You're walking down the hallway. You feel a slight breeze. What's that about? you wonder. Did someone open a window? Nope, sorry.

Your underwear is on display for the entire world to see! Embarrassing? Yes, but not so unusual. There are a number of **Embarrassing Underwear Moments** (EUMs) that are fairly common. Who hasn't lived through the accidentally hiked skirt? Or the realization that the bra you're wearing has a faulty clasp?

If the unfortunate EUM does occur in spite of your safeguards, there are ways to overcome it gracefully.

Yes, gracefully. The absolute worst way to deal with the EUM is to shriek, look embarrassed, or run around, trying to find a place to hide. All that will do is draw more attention to your exposed undies. Instead, try these comeback methods on for size.

How to Guard Against E.U.M.s

1. **More Mirror Time.** Check yourself out from every conceivable angle before venturing out into the cold, cruel world—especially when you're wearing something new.

2. **The Buddy Who's Got Your Back (Side).** Ask a friend or relative (like your sister) to preview your outfit in different kinds of light so you won't be a victim of that sneaky sun.

3. **Check with the Store Clerk.** Ask the clerk before you buy that teeny little tube thing—the one that might be a skirt, or might be a headband. If you're not sure what it is, it's a definite EUM in the making.

1. Fuhgeddabouddit! Seriously, the fastest way to put an embarrassing moment like that *behind* you is to shrug it off. Make an obvious statement like "Well, that's embarrassing!" Then fix the problem and move on. Guaranteed, everyone around you will do the same in about five minutes.

2. Make a joke. If the guy of your dreams and all his friends are standing there when you accidentally model your lingerie, just burst out laughing along with them. Everyone will think you're a totally good sport for not getting bent out of shape.

Another idea is to toss off a cool line like "What's so funny? You guys wear the same style?" Or how about "What? I was warm!" Remember: They're not laughing *at* you if they're laughing *with* you.

I was so excited about going to a new school that I chose my first-day outfit three weeks before school started. It was perfect: a cute little shirt and a matching skirt. But when I went to my first class, my English teacher, Mrs. Dunn, was wearing the exact same shirt-and-skirt set! Suddenly, my new name was Mrs. Dunn. I was so bummed.

TRAUMA -o- METER

Dressed alike. There's something about wearing the same outfit, especially on an important day or to a big event, that makes most of us uncomfortable. (Someone we know ended up wearing the same bright red designer dress as her best friend—to the senior prom! Ouch!)

First you feel as if you should be wearing a big sign that reads Not too smart. Couldn't come up with a better idea than what she's wearing! Then there's the comparison factor. **Who looks better in the outfit?** You or your clone? (And if your clone happens to be the teacher, the comparison is even more embarrassing!)

But if you're smart, you'll turn the situation to your advantage. Use it to show everyone (prom dates included) what a good sport you are—or how funny you can be. **Check out these life-saving tips.**

Three Ways to Deal When You're Wearing the Same Outfit as Someone Else

▼ If a friend cops your fashion statement, say in a mock whisper in front of your crowd, "Psst! Did you remember to wear the pink underwear set too?"

▼ Or the two of you can stand next to each other and ham it up for your friends. Strike a pose, baby—it's a fashion show!

▼ If you don't really know the person who's suddenly turned into your accidental twin (for example, your new English teacher), joke with her: "I just love what you're wearing! You have such amazing taste!"

The point is, you'll come out on top if you're able to rise above the situation.

One morning I was late for school, so I just threw on something really quickly, without even looking in the mirror. It was a new dress I had bought the night before—so what could go wrong? Plenty. Everyone stared at me all day because the dress was practically see-through. My bra and underwear were completely visible!

Wow! With embarrassing moments like that, who needs to wear blush?

When something this traumatic happens, there's only one thing to do. Face it head-on and **ask for help!** Explain the problem to your buds and ask if you can borrow a sweater or jacket from them. Or talk to one of the girls' sports coaches. Maybe she has an oversized T-shirt lying around that you could throw on over your dress for an instant layered—and thank-god-I'm-finally-clothed!—look.

Another idea is to keep a spare pair of jeans and a shirt in your locker. (You have to admit—a backup outfit could sure come in handy in a situation like this—or if you happen to get an accidental stain or tear in your clothes.)

But the bottom line is, deal with it. **Don't just walk around feeling mortified**, because the truth is, the only thing more embarrassing than showing up in a see-through dress is spending the whole day in one!

Rate Your Fashion Freakout Factor

Are you comfortable whatever you're wearing—or consumed by clothing concerns? Rate your own reaction to each of these situations on a scale of 1 to 5, using the following guidelines: 5 = want to die, 4 = seriously mortified, 3 = moderately embarrassed, 2 = no big deal, 1 = it's cool, you're laughing.

1. A cute guy from another school asks you to his school's fall homecoming dance. You arrive in a short black dress with spaghetti straps, only to find out that school tradition is to wear something long to the event. Everyone else is in floor-length gowns. You're the only one with naked legs. How embarrassed are you?

5 4 3 2 ①

2. Everyone's into skinny little tank tops this season, so you buy one and show up at a party wearing it. A friend takes you aside and quietly says, "Umm—would you like a sweater? It's kind of chilly in here." You know that she's trying to be diplomatic, but you also get what she's *really* saying: "You should *not* be wearing that top!" Are you blushing?

5 4 3 2 ①

3. You arrive at a celebration dinner for your soccer team wearing your newest baby T and a great pair of brand-new jeans. All your friends and teammates are dressed up—way up—in dresses. Do you care?

5 4 ③②1

4. You're totally out of cash this month, so you can't afford a new dress for the big dance that's coming up. You'll either have to borrow from your best bud or wear the same dress you wore last year. Can you cope? 5 4 3 2 1

5. You're spending the weekend with a new friend at her parents' summerhouse. You do a half-gainer into the pool and the straps on your bikini top snap. How embarrassed are you? 5 4 3 2 1

6. For your birthday, you get a new pair of black jeans. The next day, you wear them to school. People keep calling you "Number 9" and you have no idea why—until you get home and realize that you've forgotten to remove the size label. A big number 9 is plastered on your butt! Do you freak? 5 4 3 2 1

7. There's a hot guy at work who doesn't seem to know you're alive, so you decide to go all out. You wear a pair of form-fitting pants with a cute little sweater. Then, halfway through your shift, you bend over to pick something up and... rippppp! The pants split. How mortified are you? 5 4 3 2 1

8. On a date with your main crush, you accidentally drip nacho cheese sauce on the front of your shirt. Trying to clean it up just makes the stain worse. How embarrassed are you? 5 4 3 2 1

9. A friend is obsessing about what to wear on a hot date. You offer to let her borrow whatever she wants from your closet. "Great!" she says—until she paws through your stuff. Then she says, "Never mind. Thanks anyway," and decides to stick with her own clothes. Can you stand it? 5 4 3 2 1

Add up your answers and check out your score below.

Dress Obsessed (31–45) Clothes—and looking good in them—are top priorities for you. Be careful though. You're putting a lot of pressure on yourself to achieve perfection. Try to remember that accidents happen—sometimes you wear the "wrong" thing, and not everyone shares your taste. Cut yourself some slack and you'll be on the road to coping with life's fashion traumas when they do come along.

Model Behavior (18–30) Although you're eager to look your best whenever possible, you can handle it if you've made a fashion boo-boo. In other words, you've got a sense of proportion. You know when to laugh and when to cry. And you understand that wearing the "right" thing is sometimes just about following someone else's arbitrary rules.

Fashion Free-Spirit (9–17) You're the type who will probably end up wearing a lime-green wedding dress. You're a free spirit—a rule-breaker.

While it's great that you can laugh off almost any embarrassing situation, you could be in danger of being a bit insensitive to the feelings of others. Remember that following the dressing dos and don'ts that are connected to certain social situations is another way of showing respect for something that really matters—your friends, your family, and the people around you.

Falling into these fashion traps is one hundred percent guaranteed to increase the chances of clothing-related trauma.

❶ Sitting directly on the grass, especially if it's damp. It's not easy being green—so don't be. Put a blanket or towel down before you sit.

❷ Leaving the house without extra tampons or pads. You get the picture. Remember the Boy Scout motto and "Be prepared" by carrying reinforcements.

❸ Wearing a strapless bathing suit (or one with skinny, unreliable straps) when you dive into a pool. Do we really need to go into the physics of this one? If you plan on participating in water sports, make sure your swimsuit's got you covered.

❹ Wearing pants or skirts that are too long. Have a nice trip. See you next fall! Make sure your clothes are hemmed in the right place for you.

❺ Neglecting to scuff the bottoms of your new shoes before you go to that big event. You could end up spending the night in traction instead of on the dance floor. Swipe your soles with sandpaper before you boogie.

❻ Forgetting to wash that new, brightly colored clothing before wearing it. You could wind up with a bad case of the blues—or reds, or purples—all over your skin! Throw your clothes in a cold-water wash before you wear them.

Chapter Five

Friendship Fallout

Being a Good Friend Is a Two-way Street—and Sometimes You Run into a Major Pileup

When you were younger, the world came to a crashing halt if you were on the outs with your very best friend. Remember how it felt when she got mad because you sat with someone else on the bus? Or when she invited another girl to your sleepover?

Luckily, that's all behind you, right?

No way!

You may be light-years older, but you'll *still go* into cardiac arrest if your best friend doesn't consider you her number-one hang-out candidate.

You wonder, what does she mean by hanging out with someone else at your favorite store in the mall? And why is she suddenly studying for the big chem test with some guy—instead of you?

Friendship fallout can be totally traumatizing for two reasons. First there's **the embarrassment factor**. Then there's the *alone* factor! Who wants to spend even a week on the outs with their best buds?

So check out this chapter for all the hot tips on keeping things cool with your friends.

I've been friends with a certain girl since fourth grade, even though she's not at all popular. One day I was sitting in the caf with my other friends, and they started making fun of her. I didn't think she'd find out, so I joined in, dissing her along with everyone else and making fun of what she was wearing. Then I realized that she was sitting right behind us—and she'd heard the whole thing! I felt like a toad.

Ugh! Getting caught doing something you know is totally wrong—and realizing that you hurt someone in the process? **Personal angst and public embarrassment?** Not much is worse than that.

Being stuck in the middle of a conversation about a friend who's not there to defend herself is **totally uncomfortable.**

At that second it's so easy to just go with the flow and join in with whatever your other friends are saying. But know what? If you do, it *always* comes back to kick you in the pants.

Friendships are tricky. Sometimes it seems like the rule is: Think the way I think, do what I do, like who I like, or you're not my friend. But the truth is that your other friends will respect you more if you *don't* always chime in on their choruses.

Next time you find yourself in a situation like this one, try saying something like "Hey—she and I have been friends since forever. If you got to know her, maybe you'd like her too." Or if you don't have the guts to go that far, at least clam up and say nothing. At times like this, silence can be your best friend.

I promised my best friend that I wouldn't go after the guy she likes, but then he asked me to go to the movies. I was really into him, so I said yes, and told her I couldn't go out with her because I had cramps. I never thought she'd go to the movies without me. Wrong! She bumped into us in the theater lobby. "Wow—you got over your cramps fast," she said. Then she didn't speak to me for two weeks. Whoops!

TRAUMA
-0-
METER

"Whoops" doesn't even begin to cover this one. We are talking major trauma here.

Listen up—the number-one rule in friendships is: ***Never* steal your best friend's guy**. Not if you want your friendship to last. Sure, the saying is "All's fair in love and war"—but war is exactly what you're going to wind up with if you start chasing after your girlfriend's honey. And it can get fairly bloody.

Think about it—right now you might really have the hots for the cutie with the dimples she's been drooling over. But over the long haul, who has a better chance of being there when you walk down the aisle on your wedding day? Her or him?

Bingo! She could end up as your bridesmaid. And Dimple Boy will be nothing more than a distant memory.

Girl friendships can last for years—or even decades. Your love interests, on the other hand, last for months—or a year or two, max. So if you dump her to date him, you're risking losing someone you could have had as a friend for the rest of your life!

Is it worth it? Probably not.

Cool Rules for Friendships

▼ **DON'T** lie to your friends about anything important. (Little white lies to prevent hurt feelings are cool. It's also okay to protect your privacy— you don't have to tell your friends everything you do.)

▼ **DON'T** expect your friends to do all the giving, worrying, driving, caring, phoning, planning, or whatever. If you're really someone's friend, you have to do your share. Period.

▼ **DON'T** make your friend choose between you and someone else. Getting mad because a friend wants to spend time with someone other than you (boyfriends, girlfriends, family pets) is kindergarten stuff. Understand that your friends don't have to hang out with you 24-7.

▼ **DON'T** gossip about your friends when they're not around. It's not nice—and you wouldn't want your friends doing it to you.

▼ **DON'T** go after your friends' guys or crushes. Hands off! Always!

▼ **DO** defend your friends when other people put them down.

▼ **DO** make sure that you focus on your friends' problems at least half the time. (The other half of the time you can moan about your split ends, new zit, or impossible parents!)

▼ **DO** forgive your friends if they blow it occasionally and then have to apologize. No one's perfect.

Why Friendships Break Up

As determined by a poll of seventeen.com users

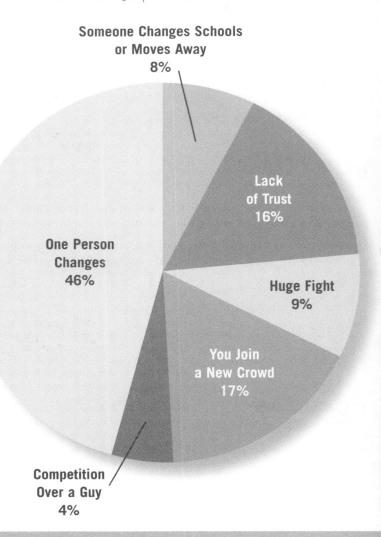

**Someone Changes Schools
or Moves Away**
8%

**Lack
of Trust
16%**

**One Person
Changes
46%**

**Huge Fight
9%**

**You Join
a New Crowd
17%**

**Competition
Over a Guy**
4%

The Party's Over

One of my best buds had a party and didn't invite me. Not only that, she'd been hanging out with people I don't really like. I decided our friendship was over, so a few weeks later I had a party and didn't invite her. The next day I ran into her mom in the grocery store and she started yelling at me in the dairy aisle, asking why I was being so cruel to her daughter. She had me trapped, and people were staring. I was really embarrassed and didn't know what to say.

TRAUMA
-O-
METER

To paraphrase a corny movie line, "Friendship means never having to say, 'Don't call me, I'll call you.'"

When you find yourself telling your mom, "Take a message," every time a certain friend calls, that's a clue that the relationship is on the downslide. And that's okay—it doesn't have to be embarrassing for either of you. The trick is to get out of it gracefully.

How to End It Gracefully When You Know a Friendship Is Over

1 Be Kind. Try to give subtle clues that let her get the message and save face. If she calls to invite you for a sleepover, say, "Oh, I think I'm going over to Jen's tonight. But thanks anyway." By the time you've turned her down four or five times, she should have figured it out.

2 Be Honest. If your bud can't or won't take the hints that you've decided to move on, just give it to her straight. Say something like "To tell you the truth, I just think we've grown apart." Or "Honestly, I can't get past the fact that you went out with Dylan when you knew I was so into him." Lay it on the line. Then the two of you can either try to work out your differences—or at the least both of you will know where you stand.

3 Be Discreet. If you've decided to end the friendship, don't dis your old pal to your new ones once the deed is done. Take the high road and keep your reasons to yourself. You'll set a great example and, with luck, your ex-friend will follow suit.

Chapter Six

Bodily Dysfunctions

How to Cope When Your Stomach Rumbles, Your Deodorant Fails, and Worse!

You're at a birthday party for a friend on a hot summer night. There are a lot of people around whom you don't know, so you're nervous. The result? Your palms are sweating so much that they feel like slabs of raw tuna—and there isn't a towel in sight.

That's when the birthday girl wants to introduce you to her older brother who's home from college. **He's gorgeous: tall, blond, and buff**, with a look in his eyes that makes you melt. He reaches out to take your hand—and you freeze. You know if you shake hands with him, you'll soak his palm.

Yuck! Instant turnoff.

So what do you do?

We know *exactly* what you do.

First, you wish you were anywhere but there. Then you wonder why **things like this never happen to the girls on Friends**. (Hint: It's a TV show, not real life.)

If you often feel like your body is betraying you, you're not alone. Luckily, we've got a zillion strategies to get you through the body blues with your dignity—and sanity—intact.

A few weeks ago I left my purse in a store at the mall. My crush and I raced all over the place, trying to find it. When we finally spotted it, we opened it to be sure it was mine—and there was my huge stash of tampons staring us in the face! I was so embarrassed, I tried to pretend it wasn't my purse, but he was totally sweet. He said, "Don't worry, I didn't see anything anyway," and gave me a smile that made me feel okay about it. What a great guy!

TRAUMA
-o-
METER

Seriously. **Don't let go of that guy!** Boys who know how to handle it when awkward moments arrive are worth their weight in gold.

Most members of the male species are not totally clueless when it comes to "that time" of the month—they know the basics from health class or sex ed. But they definitely *don't* want to be schooled about the rest. (Menstrual cramps? Tampons versus pads? Trust us, he doesn't want to know.)

If an uncomfortable moment does arise, try to remember this COOL RULE:

 **You never have to apologize for things you can't possibly control.**

And you definitely can't control when you get your period! So you shouldn't be embarrassed or feel bad if it happens when your latest crush is on the scene, or if he happens to find out your "friend" is "visiting" at the moment. [Note: No guy should get totally freaked out by this situation anyway. After all, you are a girl, and that's one of the big reasons he's attracted to you. Duh.]

Just try to avoid being uncomfortable by being prepared. Carry extra pads or tampons all the time, and avoid wearing light-colored pants at "that time of the month." Then, if an accident does happen, you'll have a better chance of being the only person who knows about it.

I was in the car with my crush and we stopped at a red light. I had been waiting for him to kiss me, and finally he did. After it was over, there was an awkward slience. It was broken when he reached into his pocket and pulled out breath mints. "Here, you need one" were the first words that marched out of his mouth. This was not exactly what I had been waiting all night to hear!

Okay, we'll admit it—the Trauma-O-Meter doesn't go high enough to handle that one. **It's a solid ten.** But here's the *good* news. There are ways to *prevent* situations like this one. All you have to do is check out the body basics tips below.

Bodily Dysfunctions How to Avoid Them

Problem	How to Avoid It
Bad breath	Before a date, or after meals, brush the back of your tongue when you brush your teeth. Dentists say that's where the bad odor originates. Also, keep breath mints handy in case you feel an attack of yuck mouth coming on.

Problem	How to Avoid It
Sweating	Believe it or not, spicy foods will make you perspire more, so steer clear of Mexican munchies and Szechuan snacks if you tend to sweat a lot.
Stomach rumblings	Eat something slightly bulky—half a bagel, for instance—before heading out to hang with your crowd. That should keep the internal noise level down.
Belching and/or passing gas	Don't eat gas-producing foods—onions, green peppers, cabbage, chocolate, heavily fried foods, and/or carbonated beverages—right before a big date or encounter with a hottie.

And remember that the COOL RULE mentioned earlier in this chapter applies to *all* bodily functions:

You never have to apologize for things you can't possibly control.

Which means that if you *do* wind up with one of those uh-oh body problems—bad breath, stomach rumblings, sweating, or passing gas (and let's hope you don't do them all at once!) you don't have to say a thing!

Actually, belching may be the one exception. Everyone knows that some burps *can* be controlled, so **people will think you're crude if you burp and say nothing**. A polite "excuse me" is a good idea if you find you've accidentally belched after scarfing down that yummy peach muffin and extra-tall cappuccino.

In P.E. class, we have to change our clothes in a really big, open locker room, and everyone can see you. All of my friends are more developed than I am, and they wear sexy lingerie from Victoria's Secret to show it off. Last week, there I was, in a cotton training bra and cotton briefs, while my friends were wearing slinky satin. Someone said, "Does your mom make you buy that underwear?" I didn't know what to say, so I just turned away and hurried to put my clothes on. Ever since then, I'm dreading getting undressed in front of my friends.

TRAUMA
-o-
METER

Girlfriend, we understand your worry—but we want you to take a deep breath for a second and focus on something important: what a terrific person you are—cleavage or no cleavage.

Let's be honest. **Boobs are cool, but they don't matter that much.** (Ever see someone not win a Nobel Prize, not get a fantastic job, or not have tons of friends because they're wearing only an A cup?)

We bet the real reason you're uncomfortable is that your friends are starting to seem older, sexier, and more confident than you feel. Luckily, there's a solution— shop until you drop!

Ditch that training bra and go for something like a Wonder Miracle Amazing enhancement bra, or if that's not your style, at least find a set of undies that makes you feel confident and sexy. That way, the next time you strip down for gym class, your locker-room traumas will totally fade away.

If, even with a new underwear set, you're *still* shy about being half naked in front your friends, **fall back on one of the quick-change tricks that girls have used for years**.

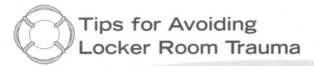

Tips for Avoiding Locker Room Trauma

▼ Go into a bathroom stall and change your top before coming back out to slip into your shorts.

▼ Change only half your clothes at a time—first the top half, switching from your blouse or sweater into your P.E. T-shirt. Then change into your gym shorts from your jeans or pants. That way you'll be exposing only half your bod at a time.

▼ Walk to a less-crowded part of the locker room – near the mirrors and sinks, for example—and quickly change there, using the need to check out your sweaty hair in the mirror as an excuse for having left the crowd.

Eavesdropping Error

A gang of girls and I went to the mall to shop for clothes. While I was in one of the dressing rooms, I heard two girls in the next booth talking about someone having a "fat ass." I popped out of the dressing room and asked them who they were dishing about. They both started giggling and blushing—and I realized they'd been gossiping about me!

TRAUMA
-o-
METER

Wow. **With friends like that, who needs this book?** You're probably getting a crash course in coping with traumas every single day!

But seriously, when you find that you're the "butt" of a joke involving either the bountiful nature of your body—or lack of curves—there are two roads to take:

❶ **The high road:** This is where you laugh it off at the moment—and seriously consider how much you want those particular friends around later. Laughing it off tells people that you are in control. You refuse to let someone else make you feel two inches tall. At least, not while they're watching anyway!

❷ **The low but still satisfying road:** This is where you talk back and let those friends know it is not cool for them to speak that way about you. Talking back lets people know that they've hurt you—and that you're not just going to let them get away with it.

No matter which road you take, at that moment you may wonder: Are your friends right? Do you have a lot of "junk in the trunk"?

Hey, that's not the point. This is: **No one has the right to put you down.** Girls who get their kicks out of making fun of others' physical appearance are usually pretty insecure about themselves. Mocking someone else's body can sometimes be a way of artificially building themselves up.

On the other hand, **guys often blurt out body comments too**. We should clue you in—this is usually just their way of getting your attention.

They'll say things like "Nice legs," or "I'd like to get my hands on *those*." What they're really saying is "I'm thinking about your bod, I find you attractive, and I don't know how else to let you know it."

Now that you know the code to deciphering these kind of guy comments, you might be tempted to see them as flattering. Don't. These comments are sexist, obnoxious, and totally politically incorrect—even if the guys saying them haven't figured that out yet.

We recommend ignoring comments like this completely—nothing hurts worse than a cold shoulder. Brrrrr.

I had a fabulous new strapless dress for the prom, and I wanted my neck and shoulders to look really great. So after I showered, I put on lots of pale, iridescent body powder, all over my shoulders, neck, and arms. When my date picked me up at home, of course we had to pose for pictures. He put his arm around me and I leaned in close. Big mistake. The whitish powder spread all over his black tux! We both started brushing at it furiously, but there was no way to get it all off before we got to the prom.

That's the trouble with powders and glitter—they look great until you wind up shedding your sparkle all over the place. Most of the time, it's cool to add a little sparkle to your face or glow to your shoulders. But for a big dance, when you want to shine your brightest? Sad to say, that's absolutely the worst time for body glamour, because that's when you'll be dancing shoulder to shoulder, cheek to cheek—and **your powder will definitely rub your date the wrong way**.

If you *do* accidentally start imitating a crop duster, apologize immediately and profusely—and then hurry to the nearest rest room to correct the situation. Try to remove the offending powder so that the next dance will leave your date holding you closer, not giving you, or your body deco, the big brush-off.

Is It Anybody's Business?

When it comes to body issues, do you let it all hang out—or keep your secrets close to the chest? Take this quiz to find out which topics you're comfortable with—and which ones you feel are too personal to tell.

For each question, figure out whom you'd share this info with. Then circle the number that corresponds to your answer. 1 = No one, 2 = Only your sister or best friend, 3 = Your girlfriends but no guy friends, 4 = Anyone who asks!

1. A bunch of friends are discussing their daily beauty routines. Someone asks you how often you shower. Whom would you tell?

1 2 ③ 4

2. You've got a strange rash "down there" and you don't know what it is. It's worrying you. Whom would you tell?

1 ② 3 4

3. You recently tried a new deodorant, and you're wondering if it works. Whom would you ask?

1 ② 3 4

4. A bunch of girls on the bus heading to the chorus competition are discussing tampons vs. pads. They ask you which you use. Whom would you tell?

1 2 ③ 4

5. A rumor is going around that you stuff your bra. It's totally not true! Okay, so maybe you did—once. Whom would you tell?

1 ② ③ 4

6. A guy you kissed made a slight face afterward and turned away, and you're afraid you have bad breath. Whom would you ask?

1 (2) 3 4

7. A gang of your friends is celebrating your sixteenth birthday, and they know you just got your driver's license. They ask to see it. You realize if you fork it over, they'll see your picture—the one with the humongous zit on your nose. Whom would you show it to?

(1) 2 (3) 4

8. You've got hair growing in some strange spots on your backside. You've tried a depilatory, but the hair grows back really fast. Whom would you tell?

1 (2) 3 4

SCORING

Add up your answers and read your score below.

Nobody's Business (8–15 points)

Other people can blab about how old they were when they got their periods, or yammer about STDs all through lunch if they want—but not you. You're very private, preferring to ask your sister to critique your new deodorant, and keeping most other body "language" to yourself. Good for you for knowing your own comfort zone. You might want to loosen up just a little though, and try confiding in at least one close friend once in a while. Sometimes it's good to get a second opinion, plus, you'll have someone to turn to if that ugly rash appears and your big sis is out of town.

Body and Soul Mates (16–24 points)

You've got great instincts for what should remain private and what's good gab session material for you and your buds. You'd tell almost anyone how often you wash your hair—what's the big deal? But when it comes to something like bad breath, you'd rather not broadcast the fact that you've been brushing your tongue after lunch! It's a great combination—being at ease in your own skin and yet realizing that not everyone wants to hear about your dandruff problems. No wonder your friends feel so comfortable talking to you!

Busy Body (25–32 points)
You're a let-it-all-hang-out type who wouldn't feel self-conscious telling a busload of Boy Scouts how to do a bikini wax. You may not be an all-out exhibitionist, but you don't have anything to hide. It's cool to be so comfortable with your bod that almost nothing embarrasses you. But try to respect the fact that not everyone feels the same way.

Chapter Seven

Party Poopers

How to Make Sure the Biggest Events of Your Life Are the Best

It's the event of the year. You want to look model-perfect, have an unbelievable time, and come home with major memories—ones that you'll want to cherish for a lifetime.

But suddenly, disaster strikes. You're totally unsure of how to act when you get there...**you've worn the wrong thing**...**three of your ex-boyfriends are there**...or your parents have ruined the party before it even had a chance to get started.

Hey—relax. It's a *party*, right? You're there for a good time, and that's what we want to make sure you have. So read on. We'll show you exactly how to manage your party jitters and ensure that no matter what **your big night is all about fun— not flubs**.

My parents agreed to let me have a party in our basement rec room and they promised to stay upstairs. Some of the guys brought bottles of booze with them and started drinking. I told them that if they didn't stop, they'd have to leave—and a lot of them did! Now my friends are riding me about being lame.

TRAUMA
-O-
METER

It's never fun to be caught between what your friends want you to do and what you think is "the right thing."

But it's totally cool that the person in this letter knew how she wanted her party to run— without alcohol—and she wasn't afraid to ask her friends to respect her wishes.

The truth is, **party guests do get out of hand sometimes**. If they do, we have some cool ways to handle the situation.

Four Steps to Having a Stress-Free Party

▼ **Make a deal with your parents ahead of time.** Tell them that if things get too wild, you'll call them in and ask for help. In exchange, they should promise to be as understanding as possible and handle the situation diplomatically—without yelling and making you and your friends feel like little kids.

▼ **Set limits with your friends in advance.** You already know you want a substance-free party—so say so from the get-go! Make it clear that alcohol or drug-related additions to the festivities will result in guests being asked to leave.

▼ **Don't invite more people than you can handle.** Enormous parties—more than twenty people—can tend to get a little crazy. Keep the numbers small if you are nervous about the event becoming too rowdy.

▼ **Plan an outdoor activity to move your group outside if its energy gets a little out of hand.** Outside, there will be less to wreck, and less of a reason for you to get stressed.

A bunch of girls organized a surprise birthday party for a popular guy in our school. All my friends were invited, but I wasn't. I didn't want to sit home alone that Saturday night, so I decided to have my own party. I invited a lot of the same people who were supposed to go to the other party, including all of my friends, but practically none of them came! Only two shy girls from my soccer team showed up. It was even more embarrassing than staying home alone that night would have been.

TRAUMA -O- METER

The conversation at school the next Monday must have been mortifying!

THEM: So—how was your party? Who came?

YOU: Uh, not many people.

THEM : Well, who?

YOU: Becca and Misty.

THEM : Yeah, and who else? It wasn't just the *three* of you, was it?

YOU: Uh, I've gotta go retake my algebra final. But this has been fun. Bye!

Hmmm. So what *should* you do if everyone on the planet gets invited to a blowout bash and you don't? Come up with an awesome alternative—something hip that you can brag about on Monday. For example, you can call a close friend, dress up, and **head out to a swanky restaurant or lounge** for a cool night out. **Or go see your favorite band in concert.**

At the very least, you can get a high-paying baby-sitting job, make a ton of money, and show up at school on Monday wearing a super cool brand-new outfit or toting the latest CDs.

The one thing you *don't* want to do is crash the party. Not when you were purposely uninvited. If you do, you'll be as welcome as chicken pox on the day before the prom.

However, there *are* times when it's okay to knock on the door asking, "Hi—can I come in?"

 ## When It's Okay to Crash

▼ **When you were invited in the first place but said you couldn't come and now your plans have changed. (This is cool if it's a casual party and the food/head count won't be seriously affected or doesn't really matter.)**

▼ **When the guy having the party passed out fliers at school. You didn't get a flier, but you've been included in his parties before.**

▼ **When your best friend was invited and was told to "bring some people along."**

▼ **When you're positive that the only reason you weren't invited is that you were out of town for the holidays, but now you're home earlier than planned, and you're ready to make the scene.**

Is it ever okay to have a party on the same night as some-one else's big bash? Sure—as long as most of your friends weren't invited to the other event. (You should never put your friends in a position where they have to choose between your party and someone else's. It's pretty selfish, which doesn't set up a good party vibe.)

So, if you know you've got at least enough guests to justify ordering more than one pizza, and cranking up the stereo sys-tem, we say go for it.

Who Invited *You?*

It was my birthday party and there were some major hotties in attendance. I decided to put some oldies on the CD player because I love beach music. I was flirting with a guy that I'd heard a lot about—he was a total babe. Just then "Twist and Shout" came on. My stepdad ran downstairs and began doing the twist in the middle of the living room—in front of all my friends, not to mention my crush. I still haven't forgiven him!

TRAUMA
-o-
METER

Parents. Sometimes they just don't get it. They don't know how—or when—to let go. They still think of you as a kid who needs them to entertain at your birthday parties. (As if.)

It's hard to get your parents to admit that you've grown up. But if you want to avoid this kind of trauma, the key is to **make your parents hip to the fact that you actually have a life of your own** (and you'd like to keep it that way).

However, as you're doing that, you might want to throw in a heavy dash of sympathy.

Now, we know what you're thinking: sympathy? When I want to strangle them?

Yeah—it's a tough gig. But your parents are feeling really weird and unsure about their role in your life right now. So keep a lid on your anger and you'll be amazed at the results.

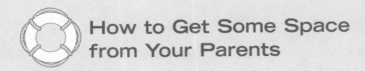

How to Get Some Space from Your Parents

Pull your parents aside if they've kicked into "intrusive mode" during a party, and deliver this speech. Do it privately—not in front of your friends—and say it very calmly and patiently:

"Dad (or Mom), I know you like to hang with my friends—and that you mean well, but I'd really like you to give us some space right now."

If that doesn't work, try asking your parents to walk in your shoes. "How would you feel if you had all your friends over for dinner, and you wanted to talk with them privately? What if *I* kept hanging around? Wouldn't that spoil your fun?"

In other words, **ask your parents to be reasonable**, and ask them in a way they can relate to. That way, they'll more than likely get the message.

My family is Presbyterian, so when I went to my first bas mitzvah, for a Jewish friend, I wasn't sure what to bring as a gift. My best friend said it was always appropriate to give money, but my parents claimed that giving cash was rude. I tried to compromise, and gave her a Blockbuster's gift certificate. But a lot of other people brought big, fancily wrapped presents, and I felt sort of embarrassed just handing her an envelope.

This is a case where two rules collide—and you get stuck in the middle.

On the one hand, it's true that it's generally not cool to give cash as a gift. On the other hand, it's always cool to stick with the customs and traditions of a given group. In the Jewish tradition, giving money for bar and bas mitzvahs is a standard, which means that it's definitely not rude.

A Blockbuster's gift certificate is a great compromise if you're not comfortable giving cash—as long as it's something your friend would actually like and use.

You can follow the Cool Rules on the next page to be sure your gift giving is always on target!

TRAUMA
-o-
METER

COOL RULES

Guide to Gift Giving

There is a ton of events you could end up invited to that you may be culturally unfamiliar with. However, if you're planning to bring a gift to any celebration, ask yourself these five questions before you make the scene, and your gift is sure to be thoughtful and appreciated.

1. **Why am I giving this gift?**

2. **Does the gift reflect my feelings for the person receiving it?**

3. **Is it something the person I'm giving it to will enjoy—as opposed to something I would enjoy?**

4. **Is it a kind gift? (Gag gifts can put you in a sticky situation if they are taken the wrong way.)**

5. **Will I feel proud to present it and have the receiver open it in front of everyone at the party?**

Last but not least, remember this basic COOL RULE: You're never *obligated* to give a gift at all. It's something you do only because you want to. That's why it's called a "gift"—not a payment!

Of course, if you don't actually *want* to give a gift, then maybe you shouldn't be going to the party in the first place.

Are You the Perfect Party Guest?

Find Out If You Have the Party Know-how That Will Put You on the Top of Everyone's Must-invite List.

1. You're invited to a senior girl's eighteenth birthday/graduation party in a fancy restaurant. It starts at seven. You:

a) don't want to be the first one there, so you arrive ten minutes late.

b) never go anywhere on time—especially parties—and will probably show up between seven-thirty and eight.

c) figure the reservation is for seven, so that's what time you'll be there.

2. A guy you know from the Ultimate Frisbee team is having a spur-of-the-moment bash on Saturday night, and he invites you. None of your girlfriends was specifically invited. You:

a) call and ask him if you can bring Amanda, your lifelong sidekick.

b) just show up with Amanda and figure he won't care.

c) go alone—it's a good opportunity to meet new people, and you can always leave early if you're not having a good time.

3. Jane, a friend from ballet class, is having a bas mitzvah and invites you. You don't really know her parents very well, so when you arrive you:

a) ignore or avoid them, and just hang out with the other dancers from your class.

b) introduce yourself to them.

c) wait for Jane to introduce you.

4. When a party's over, you:

a) go home.

b) thank the party giver and say you've had a great time.

c) offer to help clean up.

5. The cutie you've been crushing on all year shows up at your party but totally ignores you. You'd probably:

a) sulk and pout on the sidelines all night.

b) throw yourself into things and boogie your woes away.

c) flirt with his best friend to make him jealous.

6. Your best friend's parents are out of town, and she decides to throw a party. Since they're away, you see it as an opportunity to:

a) Help your friend by making sure no one gets too carried away.

b) try out some things you'd never try with parents around —like alcohol, sex, or drugs.

c) have a really fabulous time since no adults are watching.

7. You notice that a few shy girls are just hanging by themselves at a party. You:

(a) sit and talk to them for a few minutes, and try to introduce them to a friend or two of yours.

b) casually mention to them that a bunch of people are about to start watching *Titanic* in the family room. You figure that maybe they'll be more comfortable in a low-key atmosphere.

c) make fun of them in hushed tones to your friends, and quietly ask the host why she invited them to begin with.

8. You and your friends are underage, but someone brings a case of beer to your friend's party anyway. You:

a) join right in and grab a brew.

b) don't care what other people do, but stick to Diet Coke yourself.

(c) stay on your toes, for your friend's sake, and keep an eye out for drunk and disorderly behavior.

SCORING

Add up your answers and read your scores.

1. (a)2 (b)1 (c)3
2. (a)2 (b)1 (c)3
3. (a)1 (b)3 (c)2
4. (a)1 (b)2 (c)3
5. (a)2 (b)3 (c)1
6. (a)3 (b)1 (c)2
7. (a)3 (b)2 (c)1
8. (a)1 (b)2 (c)3

Best Guest (20–24 points)

You're on everyone's A list because you've figured out what the party's all about. It's about making sure everyone has fun—which means showing up on time (so the host doesn't freak and think no one's coming). Or introducing yourself to your friend's parents if you've never met them before. Or offering to help clean up. Keep up the good work, and maybe your party poise will rub off on your friends. (Wouldn't you love it if someone helped you get rid of those pizza boxes once in a while?)

Gala Gal (14–19 points)

You may not follow every nitpicky rule to the letter, but your friends have zero complaints about you. You're the type who knows how to have fun, liven things up, and still be considerate of others. You know that technically it's not considered cool to bring uninvited guests to a party—but the guy on your Ultimate Frisbee team would be bummed if you didn't bring your best friend along. Just to be sure though, you call and ask. Give yourself extra points for understanding that what really matters in social situations is that everyone feels at ease.

Party Harder (8–13 points)

Your definition of a party: a place to have a blowout good time no matter what. You definitely know how to make an entrance—but do you know how to cope if the party's a bust? Not really. If things don't go your way, you beat a hasty retreat. Or maybe your me-first frame of mind has contributed to the early breakup of a party or two.

Feel weird about that? Then at the very next party you're at, try showing up with a tray full of cookies, or offering to help pick up at the end of the event. And don't let yourself get totally out of control. You'll be amazed at how many more invites you get in the coming months.

Chapter Eight

Tough Times

How to Cope, and Avoid Embarrassment, When Life Gets Truly Traumatic

There's probably nothing that registers more pain and embarrassment on your own personal Richter scale than **hurting someone's feelings when they're already going through a crisis or difficult time**. But we've all done it: said the wrong thing to someone in the hospital, blundered into **a foot-in-mouth moment** with someone whose parent just lost his or her job, or worse.

Times like that are when you really need COOL RULES. Then, even if your instincts are not the best, at least you'll have your instruction sheet to get you through.

Illness and Death

A friend's mother died unexpectedly. I went to the funeral with some other friends, but our friend was crying so much, we didn't know what to say to her. Finally, we just left without saying anything. Afterward, we felt stupid for having done that.

TRAUMA -O- METER

Your instincts weren't totally off here. It might not have helped to say anything to your friend while she was sobbing with grief.

But there are two things you could have done that would have been appreciated, and kept you from feeling embarrassed and awkward.

First, you could have simply gone up to your friend and, without saying anything, given her a hug. **(Actions really can speak louder than words sometimes.)**

Or, if you're not a natural-born hugger, you could have waited for her to compose herself, then approached her to **say the few words that are always right in those situations**: "I am so sorry."

Often, people are reluctant to say those four words because they don't seem like enough. How can "I am so sorry" possibly help when your friend has lost someone so close to her? The answer is it's the gesture that counts, not the words themselves. Being there for your friend means everything; it means that even though she's lost one of the most important people in her life, she's not alone. Her friends will be there for her. That's what you want to convey.

What Else Can You Do When There's a Serious Illness or Death in the Family of One of Your Friends?

▼ **Offer to help.** Maybe the family needs baby-sitting assistance. Maybe you can drive them somewhere, or pick up the dry cleaning. Let your friend know that she/he can call on you anytime, and you'll do whatever you can to help.

▼ **Bring food.** Your friend's family may not have the time, energy, or interest to cook, so you can help out by putting something appetizing in front of them. When you bring the dish over, you can visit, but only if you get the feeling that your presence is welcome. In a situation like this, your friend and his or her family may simply need to be alone.

▼ **Send a note.** If one of your friend's relatives is sick or dies, write a note to your friend expressing your concern, or sympathy, to the whole family. If the family member has passed away, it's especially meaningful if you can remember a special quality you liked about the person who's gone, and mention it. But what you actually say isn't the important part—you've simply got to add your voice to the many who are saying "We love you, and we care about this difficult time you are having."

Family Crises

My dad lost his job and we've been on a tight budget ever since. My friends don't seem to realize it though. They keep suggesting expensive activities like shopping sprees and skiing trips. I'm too embarrassed to admit I can't afford it.

TRAUMA -O- METER

Whether it's a change in family income, impending divorce, or another kind of emotional stress at home, you can't expect your friends to be sensitive and supportive if you don't tell them what's going on.

So, first, tell them you need some extra consideration right now, and explain why. And try to remember that what you're going through is probably *not* permanent. Your dad could get another job soon, so **hang in there**.

Divorce is a little different. When your parents split, it often results in bigger lifestyle changes—and they *can* have long-lasting effects.

On the other hand, you may not be the first person in your crowd to go through this, so **turn to your friends for advice**. Make it clear that you don't want their pity—but you wouldn't mind a little girlfriend attention and an extra dose of sympathy while your life is being turned upside down. If they've been there, they'll know what to say.

When it's your turn to offer support for your buds, it's important to think through what you say before you open your mouth to say it. Here's a guide to help get you through the toughest times.

How to Handle Your Most Difficult Situations

Difficult Situation	The Right Thing to Say
Your friend's parent or sibling is seriously ill	"Do you want to talk about it?" or "I'll be here for you to help you get through this."
Your friend's family member dies	To your friend: "I love you and I'm totally here for you. Call me anytime you want to talk, day or night." To her other family members: "I'm so sorry. Let me know if there's anything I can do."
Your friend's parents are nearing divorce	"That sucks. I'm totally sorry this is happening to you." (Or some other simple-yet-direct expression of sympathy.)
Your friend is seriously ill	"I'll help you through this however I can."
Your friend is having trouble dealing with a parent's problem (such as alcoholism or drug addiction)	"I'll help you find a counselor you can talk to about this." (See the end of this chapter for phone numbers giving confidential referrals to counselors in your area.) or "You can always come stay at my house if things at your place get too intense."
Your friend's family income takes a turn for the worse	"This must be really difficult right now, but things will get better. Until then, who needs cash when we've got MTV?"

A Friend in Need

My buds and I noticed that someone we hung out with in school was losing weight rapidly. Then I found out that she actually had an eating disorder. She was going to counseling for it and everything!

Now, whenever I try to talk to her, I don't know what to say. I know I must seem like such a jerk!

TRAUMA
-o-
METER

Probably one of the toughest things to deal with is a friend who is in serious trouble. Whether someone is depressed, gravely ill, has a problem with alcohol or drugs, or, as in the case above, has an eating disorder, it's easier to tell what's happening on the outside of a person than what's happening on the *inside*.

Luckily, there are some outside signals that can let you know when something is wrong.

It's very likely that a friend in trouble will undergo a drastic change in her dress, appearance, habits, or attitude. Here's a two-part Cool Rule to follow if you notice this kind of change in one of your friends.

What to Do When You Suspect Your Friend's in Trouble

1. **Grab your friend during a quiet moment, or take her aside and ask seriously if she is okay.** Then listen closely to the answer. Maybe she'll explain that she's trying a new style, or just tired from watching too much late-night TV. But if something actually is wrong, you may be able to pick up a slight hesitation in your friend's voice. Or her response may be overly enthusiastic—and smack of total denial.

2. **Whatever response you get, don't pressure your friend for more info about her situation.** Just let her know that if something *is* troubling her, you're around to talk to. Let her know that your ear is always available because you're concerned. Your friend may open up to you. Or at least she may feel more comfortable with the idea of talking to someone about what's bothering her.

Worst-Case Scenario

What happens when showing you care doesn't seem to help matters? When you suspect your friend's problem is getting worse and worse?

Sometimes, your best option is to put matters into someone else's hands. Someone who could actually step in and take an active role in helping your friend.

It may feel creepy at the time, but *do* tell your parents, your friend's parents, your friend's older brother or sister, or a school counselor (choose the person most likely to get through to your friend) about what you suspect is wrong.

Hey, you may feel bad if your friend accuses you of butting in, but not as bad as you would if you could have done something to help—and decided not to.

For free, confidential referrals to counselors in your area, call any of these toll-free numbers:

General
National Youth Crisis Hotline
800-448-4663 (24 hours)

Drug Abuse
DrugHelp National Helplines Network
800-378-4435

National Drug and Alcohol Treatment Hotline
800-662-HELP

Child Abuse/Domestic Abuse
National Child Abuse Hotline
800-422-4453

National Domestic Violence Hotline
800-799-SAFE

Suicide/Runaways Adolescent
Crisis Intervention and Counseling Nineline
800-999-9999 (24 hours)

National Runaway Switchboard and Suicide Hotline
800-621-4000 (24 hours)

Eating Disorders
Eating Disorders Awareness and Prevention
800-931-2237

Harvard Eating Disorders Center
888-236-1188

The Renfrew Center
800-RENFREW

Mental Health
National Institute of Mental Health Anxiety Disorders Education Program
888-826-9438

Rape/Sexual Abuse
RAINN – Rape, Abuse, Incest National Network
800-656-HOPE (24 hours)

Voices In Action
800-7-VOICE-8

Self-Injury
SAFE Alternatives (Self Abuse Finally Ends) at Rock Creek Center
800-DON'T-CUT

Sexuality
National Gay and Lesbian Hotline
888-THE-GLNH

Chapter Nine

Do I Know You?

How to Cope with Parents, Siblings, and Other Relatives When You'd Rather Deny Their Existence

Would you rather go to school with hat hair for a week than be seen in public with your parents? Is your kid sister so geeky, you've actually considered entering the witness relocation program so that you won't ever have to hang out with her again?

Not a surprise.

Family members can be...errr...challenging to be around. But, believe it or not, **there are ways to cope when your relatives are less than fabulous**—ways that could keep things at home a little more peaceful.

Keep reading and find out the secret for stress-free socializing with your sibs, 'rents, and other relatives.

My mom took me on a trip to the Bahamas—just the two of us. While I was suntanning on the beach, two guys from my school walked by. As I was talking to them, I noticed that they stopped paying attention to me. They were looking up the beach toward my mother, walking toward us. She was topless! I was so embarrassed, I ran back to our room to hide.

TRAUMA -O- METER

Folks, we have a winner! This trauma is so awful, it's completely off the charts—and it's **our vote for trauma of the year**! Yuck!

Okay—now that we've gotten a hold of ourselves, let's talk about the problem at hand: your mom—no shirt—and guys from your school whom you like. Why would any mom do this? Could be a dozen reasons, but that really isn't the point.

The point is that your mom was inconsiderate of you and your feelings. It's more or less your mom's prerogative to sunbathe in the buff, but she definitely could have told you she was planning on doing it beforehand.

That would have given you a chance to object if the idea made you uncomfortable. Or, at least, you could have steered your friends away from the scene if you knew your mom was due to join you *au naturel* at any second.

Parents need to have good manners too, and they know it. But sometimes they forget. You can often clue them in by simply asking them to put themselves in your shoes.

How would your mom like it if you removed your top in front of an adult *she* knew? If Mom argues that it's not the same thing, simply try to explain to her—in a calm, rational manner—that it *feels* the same to you.

The trick here is to **keep your cool**. If you *talk* rather than yell or complain, she's more likely to listen. Simply ask her to try to show you the same respect she wants you to show her. It's a reasonable request.

(For more tips on how to get your parents to shape up, see **Four Steps to Getting Rid of Your Parents When Your Friends Are Around,** on page 115.)

Every time my friends come over, my little sister hangs around and talks with the guys. She laughs at all their jokes and bats her eyes and stuff. It's almost like she's flirting with them! It's so weird because she's only ten years old—and I can't think of any way to stop her from doing it!

That's rough, and the worst part is, you might not be able to stop your sister's behavior. Why not? Because you can't possibly offer her something she wants in exchange for her disappearing act. She's already getting what she wants—big sister time!

Honestly, hanging out with you and your friends is her main goal. And the way she's acting is probably her attempt to be as cool and grown-up as you are.

So, on the one hand, **chill a little** and try to see the way your sister is acting as a compliment. She wants to be like you and have friends like yours, which is a nice thing.

Then try to **minimize your embarrassment factor** by learning to laugh the whole thing off. Chances are that's what your guy friends are doing anyway.

Rate Your Parents—
How Embarrassing Are They?

Are your folks really that bad? Take this quiz and find out.

1. When your friends drop by your house unexpectedly on a Saturday night, your parents:

a) clear out of the family room so you can take over the space.

b) start popping popcorn and offering everyone something to drink.

c) quiz your friends endlessly about their favorite classes and how they're doing in school this term.

2. When your dad drops you off at school in the morning, he:

a) lets you drive, so your friends can see you pulling up at school.

b) tries to act casual about it, but secretly watches to see who you're hanging out with and how you behave.

c) gets out of the car and has a ten-minute conversation with some other carpooling parents.

3. Your mom's wardrobe:

a) is in style and fashionable compared to other moms, yet looks appropriate for her age.

b) looks a lot like yours.

c) hasn't changed in ten years.

4. You're at the beach on vacation with your parents. They:

a) give you plenty of space to hang out with new friends, and let you eat your meals with those friends if you want.

b) join a game of beach volleyball with a bunch of teens and make killer spike shots at the net.

c) beg you to let them bury you in the sand up to your neck like they did when you were five.

5. If your parents accidentally pick up the phone while you're talking on another extension, they usually:

a) apologize and hang up immediately so you can keep talking.

b) ask you how much longer you'll be and launch into an explanation about why they need the phone.

c) yell at you for being on the phone so much.

6. If your dad walks in while you're smooching with your honey, he:

a) turns around and leaves.

b) says, "Oh, sorry—but are you kids done with the popcorn and butter in the kitchen, because you left it out."

c) has a fit and lectures you about how you shouldn't be "getting involved" at your age.

7. When your boyfriend of four months comes over for dinner, the topic of conversation will probably be:

a) the usual—school news, complaints about work, and a little bit of chitchat about your boyfriend's basketball victories.

b) the MTV awards—your dad is a fanatic.

c) the time your guy wrecked his parents' car last month—your parents want to know all the details.

8. When you got a C minus on the Spanish midterm, your parents:

a) asked you if there was anything they could do to help.

b) hired a tutor.

c) immediately called the school to complain that the test was too hard.

SCORING

Count up the number of A, B, and C answers to find out which parent profile fits your dear-old-mom-and-dad.

Parents for Prez! (4 or more A answers)

Your parents are absolutely excellent—cutting you slack when you need it and showing you respect and support when times are tough. They know better than to try to be your best buds—which makes you feel even closer to them. Figure out a way to clone these gems, and share them with the rest of the world!

Good As It Gets (4 or more B answers)

For the most part, your parents are cool. They're warm and fuzzy with your friends and they don't create too many miserably mortifying moments for you. Once in a while your parents may try too hard, but their hearts are in the right place. So if you've got some issues with them, maybe you could try having a talk. They'll probably listen.

Parentalis Prehistoricus (4 or more C answers)

Uh-oh. Your parents are in a class by themselves, and we feel your pain. They obviously love you truly, madly, deeply, but they definitely haven't figured out how to show that they trust and respect you as well. The result: more mortifying moments than most people are genetically programmed to withstand—and you're seriously considering putting yourself up for adoption! Assuming you've actually earned their trust and respect, you might want to have a carefully planned heart-to-heart with your parents and let them know how you feel.

So, your friends are on their way to your house for a party and your parents sure don't look like they're going anywhere. What's a girl to do? Check out the Life Saver below.

Four Steps to Getting Rid of Your Parents When Your Friends Are Around

❶ Ask. Pick a time when things are calm—when you're not fighting or screaming at each other—and ask your parents nicely if they could give you some private time with your friends.

❷ Explain. Make sure your parents understand that you're not trying to do anything they'll disapprove of. You just want some privacy, so you and your friends can relax. Ask them to imagine how they'd feel if *you* were hanging around, listening to their conversations, every time they had adult friends over.

❸ Negotiate. If they're still crowding you, tell your parents you'll make a deal. You want more time alone with your friends—but what do *they* want? Maybe they want you to clean your room more often, or spend some time with your grandmother, or stop giving them "that look." Be willing to fulfill some of their needs in exchange for getting what you want. Come up with a fair trade, and then keep up your end of the bargain.

4 *Back off.* If asking, explaining, and negotiating don't work, try giving in. One evening let them hang out and talk to your friends as much as they want. (We swear, you can stand it for one night!) It'll seem like an eternity to you, but eventually your parents will leave. And if they don't, they'll see that you and your buds are really just hanging—and you'll build some trust, which should make it easier to get rid of them next time.

Afterword

Now that you've scoped out all the letters in this book, you're probably thinking, Hey—my life's not so bad after all. And guess what? You're absolutely right. At least now you know how to handle it if things *do* get traumatic or suddenly start to spin out of control.

You've got COOL RULES to get you through even the grossest body incident, the clumsiest whoops-there-goes-the-ketchup moment, or the most tongue-tying conversation mishap.

Oh—we have one last rule to keep in mind. **Nobody's perfect.** The only thing more embarrassing than trying to achieve perfection is being naïve enough to think that it's possible!

So get out there! Have fun! And resolve to be your own cool, cute, sometimes-quirky self. Your true friends will absolutely appreciate you for it!

Free gift from Neutrogena

To get a great deal on a subscription to

seventeen

magazine
and a FREE gift from
Neutrogena,
log on to
www.enews.com/
seventeenbook.
Or call
800-388-1749
and mention
code 5BKA7

seventeen

BOOKS...
FOR THE TIMES OF
YOUR LIFE

0-06-440871-X

How to Be Gorgeous
The Ultimate Beauty Guide to
Makeup, Hair, and More
By Elizabeth Brous, former beauty director of **seventeen**
Seventeen's guide to looking glam includes:
- Awesome makeup tips
- Secrets for healthy, gorgeous skin and hair
- Ways to find the best look for you—
  without spending a fortune
- And much, much more!

Don't delay! It's your turn to be gorgeous!

0-06-447235-3

The Boyfriend Clinic
The Final Word on Flirting,
Dating, Guys, and Love
By Melanie Mannarino, senior editor of **seventeen**
Do you have questions about love and relationships?
Relax—**seventeen**'s got you covered.
With answers to such questions as:
- How do I get a boyfriend?
- Is he the right guy for me?
- How do I know it's really love?

It's your love guide—now put it to work!

0-06-440872-8

Total Astrology
What the Stars Say About
Life and Love
By Georgia Routsis Savas
Here's your cosmic connection to
all the signs in the zodiac.

For help answering your
deepest questions—look to the stars!

AN EXCITING FICTION SERIES FROM

Seventeen

LOOK FOR A NEW TITLE EVERY MONTH!

They're ready for life. They're ready for love.
They're *Turning Seventeen.*

Follow four high-school heroines—Kerri, Jessica, Erin, and Maya—during the most exciting time of their lives. There's love, friendship, and huge life decisions ahead. It's all about to happen—just as they're *Turning Seventeen.*

KERRI

JESSICA

MAYA

ERIN

Available wherever books are sold.

Books created and produced by Parachute Publishing, LLC., distributed by HarperCollins Children's Books, a division of HarperCollins Publishers.
© 2000 PRIMEDIA Magazines, Inc., publisher of **seventeen**. **Seventeen** is a registered trademark of PRIMEDIA Magazines Finance Inc.